Rabbit and Turtle Go to School

Rabbit and Turtle Go to School

Lucy Floyd
Illustrated by Christopher Denise

Green Light Readers
Harcourt, Inc.
Orlando   Austin   New York   San Diego   London

"Let's race to school," said Rabbit.

"You ride the bus and I'll run.

On your mark, get set, *go*!"

Rabbit ran fast.
He went up the mountain.

Turtle got on the bus.
The bus left.

Rabbit ran very fast.
He ran down the mountain.

The bus stopped.

Rabbit ran very, very fast.
He was almost there.

The bus stopped again.

Rabbit stopped for a snack.

Turtle's bus drove by Rabbit

and on to school.

"Let's race tomorrow," said Turtle. "I'll give you a head start."

Draw a Map!

Rabbit and Turtle each went to school a different way. How do you go to school?

WHAT YOU'LL NEED

 paper

 crayons or markers

1. Look carefully at the main places you see on your way to school.

2. Notice where each place is.

3. Draw your map.

Share your map with a friend!

Meet the Illustrator

Christopher Denise likes drawing animals. Before he starts to draw, he looks at pictures of real animals to get ideas. He says, "I know children will like a story even more if the animals are really special."

Christopher Denise

For information about permission to reproduce selections from this book,
Please write Permissions, Houghton Mifflin Harcourt Publishing Company
215 Park Avenue South NY NY 10003.

www.hmhco.com

First Green Light Readers edition 2000
Green Light Readers is a trademark of Harcourt, Inc., registered in the
United States of America and/or other jurisdictions.

The Library of Congress has cataloged an earlier edition as follows:
Floyd, Lucy.
Rabbit and turtle go to school/Lucy Floyd; illustrated by Christopher Denise.
p. cm.
"Green Light Readers."
Summary: Rabbit and Turtle reenact their
famous race while they are on their way to school.
[1. Fables. 2. Folklore.] I. Denise, Christopher, ill. II. Title.
PZ8.2.F57Rab 2000
[398.2]—dc21 99-50804
ISBN 978-0-15-204811-2
ISBN 978-0-15-204851-8 (pb)

SCP 15 14 13 12 11
4500507193

Ages 4-6
Grade: 1
Guided Reading Level: E
Reading Recovery Level: 8

Green Light Readers
For the reader who's ready to GO!

"A must-have for any family with a beginning reader."—*Boston Sunday Herald*

"You can't go wrong with adding several copies of these terrific books to your beginning-to-read collection."—*School Library Journal*

"A winner for the beginner."—*Booklist*

Five Tips to Help Your Child Become a Great Reader

1. Get involved. Reading aloud to and with your child is just as important as encouraging your child to read independently.

2. Be curious. Ask questions about what your child is reading.

3. Make reading fun. Allow your child to pick books on subjects that interest her or him.

4. Words are everywhere—not just in books. Practice reading signs, packages, and cereal boxes with your child.

5. Set a good example. Make sure your child sees YOU reading.

Why Green Light Readers Is the Best Series for Your New Reader

• Created exclusively for beginning readers by some of the biggest and brightest names in children's books

• Reinforces the reading skills your child is learning in school

• Encourages children to read—and finish—books by themselves

• Offers extra enrichment through fun, age-appropriate activities unique to each story

• Incorporates characteristics of the Reading Recovery program used by educators

• Developed with Harcourt School Publishers and credentialed educational consultants